TITLE
An unenthusiastic lover

Chapter 1

The Border Guard

Jaecar, the fiercest of the Border Guards, sat tight for me outside my hovel.

I met him there. After such a long time, I was unafraid of him notwithstanding his scary air and athletic form.

He had sparkling dark hair and characterized muscles firmly winding his body under his calfskin tunic and breeches. Common blade resting in its hip sheath.

He'd never given me cause for concern. In spite of that I realized the guys checked out him apprehensively.

For what reason wouldn't they?

He'd outsmarted them regularly enough in the preliminary rings. The main genuine rivalry for our young Alpha, Draven.

"Allow me to see." He held out his hand eagerly.

My sketchbook.

It was anything but an inquiry.

I gave it over, as I generally did. Happy to impart my work to him.

He generally needed to see what new scrawls I'd done.

"Is this Warlock Creek?" He highlighted one page.

"Indeed. That is my cherished spot."

"Ok, yes." He gestured. "In the old oak tree."

I grinned up at him. "Definitely. You know me so well."

"I ought to at this point, shouldn't I?" He ran a hand through his smooth dark hair. Dull foreheads floating over thickly lashed green eyes. Eyes which appeared to consistently find everything.

I'd generally asked why he was my companion. He was so striking and I was so plain.

I had strawberry light hair. Also was ghastly white rather than brilliant tan like different females in our pack.

However there aren't a considerable lot of us altogether.

"How's your pursuing going?" I took my sketchbook back before he saw the page I'd canine eared toward the back.

A portrayal of his unusual wanderer eyes.

"Not well, I'm apprehensive." He gave me a curious look.

"Why? How should she not be keen on you?" I prodded. I'd perceived how the six females in our pack took a gander at him. However females were scant and leary of the forceful guys, they all cast him yearning looks.

In light of current circumstances.

He resembled a cut sculpture. Were I not far underneath his association and reluctant to turn out to be any male's property, he'd have been my decision.

"Great inquiry." He said boredly.

Who is it? I pondered not interestingly. Going over them six to me. I'd never seen him give any of them a fascinated eye.

"Will you let me know which one it is?" I watched two of them crawling carefully through the town. Stealthily checking out corners.

In light of current circumstances.

A significant number of the Asara Pack Males were known to be exceptionally physically forceful this season.

Capricious and hazardous for an unexpecting female.

"The Full Moon is coming." I commented looking up.

The Mating Moon.

At the point when every one of the guys would need to use their virile necessities on female reproducer bodies.

Like mine.

Chapter 2
Fear of the Mating Moon

It's an alarming season.

However, four years prior, when my dad had passed, Jaecar had assisted me with transforming my cabin into an invulnerable fortification. As strong as the Asara domain line dividers he'd helped fabricate.

"Indeed it is." He checked out me consistently.

"How would you oppose it?" I pondered so anyone might hear. I'd never seen him be forceful with anybody. It was essential for the explanation I confided in him.

"I don't. Not completely. It makes me hot for all that moves." He conceded.

I snickered however he gave me a brief glance.

"Not especially entertaining, Sam."

"Fine." I shrugged. "You hungry?"

He lifted an eyebrow and I energetically elbowed him.

"For food! Not whatever female has you tied more tight than a catch rope." I gestured toward the two ladies.

He has been seriously irritable of late. Frequently appearing to be eager with me and following off.

He was never similar to that.

He gave me a long look prior to proposing. "Indeed. We should go get those Elderberries you favor."

I gestured. Radiating up at him.

We talked about pack tattle.

I watched him insightfully. He gazed at the sun moving off the twining spring somewhere out there. Birds peeped in the brush of trees encompassing the two sides of the water.

Yet, my oak tree was the most elevated. I looked at it fondly. It was empty in the middle with an enormous opening where it'd endured. Still it was tall, strong and proudful.

Like Jaecar. My look got back to his profile.

He was thoughtful today. Notwithstanding his standard seriousness, with me he was regularly energetic.

Aside from of late.

I hung over and sprinkled water from the rivulet onto him.

He threw water back at me.

Before long I was chuckling boisterously. Occupied with the play.

He gently handled me.

I spilled onto the leaves. His hand supporting the rear of my head and my back to hold me back from getting injured as he brought down onto me.

He moved all the more serenely over me and his face became genuine.

I knew promptly something had changed.

"We should examine something, Samantha."

My complete name? He possibly utilizes that when he's actual grave.

"What?" I grimaced up into his puncturing green eyes.

"This evening and this evening the pack will look for mates."

Indeed, under the Mating Moon.

"I know." I gestured energetically. "My cabin is built up recollect? You assisted me with making it impervious."

"Indeed I did." He made a sound as if to speak and looked to the leaves to the side me.

"Relax, Jaecar. I'll secure myself. I'll be protected."

"No, Samantha." His look arrived on me levelly. "You will not."

Chapter 3

His Decision

"What do you mean?" My foreheads drew together in stress.

"You're not returning to your cottage during the mating this evening."

"Indeed. I'm." I said all the more immovably. "When we leave here, I'm going."

"No." His strong green look consumed into me and my stomach sank. "I've picked you for my mate."

What?

I attempted to throw him off yet I was a seemingly insignificant detail and he was probably the most grounded male in the pack. One of the boundary watches.

What supplication did I need to unstick him?

Abruptly, getting over here each day with him appeared to be extremely perilous. What had I been thinking?

He was watching feelings pour over my face. Pausing.

"You can't simply do that!" Determination locked my jaw.

"I as of now have. I've tricked you out of your hovel and I have you. What's more when it's mating time this evening, I'll spill my wolf seed in you and imprint you as mine."

The Hell you will! I glared fervently at him.

"You can't!" I voiced my protest.

He must be kidding!

The Jaecar I knew could never direct such sentiments toward me!

"I can." His mouth brightened. "What's more I will. On the off chance that I don't another person will."

I shook my head, declining to tune in. Who are you?

He murmured. "You've gone excessively long without a mate, Samantha. How since a long time ago did you figure the pack would represent it?"

I went to push him off yet he wouldn't move.

Feeling to some degree froze I started hitting his shoulders with my clench hands. "Get off of me!"

He got my wrists and stuck them over my head in one of his huge hands. "Be sensible, Sam. There are almost forty wolves in our pack. Also there are you seven females of reproducing age. Some of you won't just be taken this evening, however must be imparted to numerous guys to keep pack harmony."

"For what reason would you do this to me?" I flickered at him in shock. "It's me!"

"I know. That is the reason I'm reluctant to share..."

"Jaecar!" I protested. Battling against his viselike hold.

"Shh..." He murmured nearly against my lips. "I could've not told you. I could've kept you around here until some other time and just taken you when the moon released my monster."

Chapter 4

Hole in a Tree

He followed a finger down my cheek with his free hand. "Yet, out of graciousness to you, I'm telling you what'll occur in a couple of brief hours."

I was stunned when Jaecar sat up and loosened up a long length of rope from around his midriff.

I battled in truth then, at that point. "You're not tying me up!"

He rose and bounced with on leg on each side of my hips, rope close by. Ready to tie me.

I accepting his development as a chance, and as he jumped up I slide down between his legs before he dropped his weight. Utilizing my enormous adaptability to crease back onto my feet and stagger into a run.

My sketchbook clunked to the overgrown timberland floor. Deserted as I ran. Controlling along the wide spring. So unglued, I missed the restricted scaffold.

He's acquiring on me. He was enormous and quick. As one of the line monitor, his body was very much sharpened to tenaciously once-over gatecrashers.

We'd hustled ordinarily and I realized he'd before long be surpassing me in the event that I didn't accomplish something. Swiping up a weighty piece of wood I pivoted and flung it at him.

It surprised him. Hitting him in the center and thumping the air from him. Compelling him to respite and grasp his stomach as he heaved for air.

I exploited the headstart and ran until tracking down one of my other most loved trees An old cottonwood. I got a low branch and tucked my feet. Swinging my body in a curve and into the empty close to the branch. Dropping down into the tree.

The opening was sufficiently high above me, there'd be no getting me out of this one without my help. Dissimilar to the oak, this one was excessively restricted. I preferred spots like this where I could wedge in the tree by spreading my knees and elbows and afterward sketch from the tree window, concealed by any interlopers.

I never suspected I'd stow away from Jaecar.

Later a couple of seconds of quiet, I shimmied up within the tree to simply peer over the lower part of the opening.

He was remaining in the woods. Gradually looking at the trees. "I know you're here, Samantha. I will track down you You can't stow away from me."

Indeed, I can.

"Remember who I am." He reminded. "I routinely overview things undeniably more considerable then you."

Not today, Jaecar.

"Come out!" He yapped fretfully.

I jolted at the telling note in his voice. Enticed to arise. Detecting the outcome of his mounting outrage would be high.

"I could be delicate with you. Kind. Yet, assuming you make me work for it..."

I looked out the opening again and saw him gradually pivoting to check the trees.

"Then, at that point, it'll be you that experiences the craving I've worked in looking for you..."

Chapter 5

Waiting Me Out

Want the tissue he implies. My heart was droning so hard I dreaded he'd hear it. Be that as it may, the tree was thick and great at covering such sounds.

"Samantha!" He yapped. "Have it your way! Be that as it may, remember it's me. I have a deep understanding of you. There's no place you can go, no place you can conceal that I will not before long find you..."

He's right. He knows a lot about me.

How is it that I could be so thoughtless? Absurd, silly young lady! I reviled myself.

My stomach snarled and I winced. Supporting a hand to it and pausing my breathing for dread his head would fly through the opening and request I come out.

I will not. I chose at that moment. Furthermore he can't get me out.

I sat in that tree until long later I realized he'd gone. He'd probably be backtracking to check around my hovel. He'd frequently let me know frightened animals will commonly run home at the main chance. Which implies that is the place where he'll be pausing.

My stomach snarled once more. What's more my cheeks puffed as I paused my breathing in alarm.

Nothing. I was protected.

I recollected that we'd examined the elderberries before yet never gone. I haven't eaten since yesterday.

What's more with the Mating Moon, my hunger would be going all out. Then, at that point, my stomach will truly start snarling.

I expected to get food in my midsection or stowing away would be no utilization. It was awful sufficient that my female fragrance would be elevated with the moon's rising. Sending every one of the guys into a sexual furor.

They'd destroy the tree to observe me, when the moon was at full tallness, on the off chance that they discovered my stomach snarling.

I crawled up to peer from the empty. Nothing.

I slipped from it like being conceived. Serpenting to the ground prior to allowing my toes to unfasten from the edge and drop me to my hands. I moved to my feet and glanced around carefully.

No Jaecar.

In the tree, a few branches over the empty, Jaecar was hunkered on an appendage. Elbows supported on his knees as he hung tight for me to come out.

Knowing he'd not have the option to haul me out of this specific tree. He whirled a leaf behind his fingertips. Allowing it to drift down behind the tree once he saw me twining from the entry. He prepared himself on the branch. Prepared to jump down. Yet, realizing surprising me too fast would simply drive me back into this tree or another.

He was a shadow behind me as I forewent the elderberry shrubs, realizing it was conceivable he'd lay on pause there as well.

Chapter 6
His Ensnarement

I went directly toward a remain of bushes where I had a little snap box tucked under, loaded up with dried meat for eating as I actually look at my snares. I grabbed a modest bunch and heard the pallet of something weighty and felt something get my lower leg.

I peered down as I was drug a distance. Beginning to be utilized up was just halted by Jaecar's clench hand getting the rope and holding it down. Holding the enormous trunk behind him back from overturning down and leaving me swinging.

Simple prey for the pack later.

Kindly don't. I sent him an arguing look. Earthy colored eyes colossal with franticness.

"H-how'd you know?" I shouted.

He shrugged. "You'd not return to the cabin. Since you realized it'd be the primary spot I'd look. So I killed that from potential outcomes. I realized you'd in any case be ravenous however wouldn't go to the elderberry brambles since we'd examined them toward the beginning of today. That left just a single other prepared inventory of food. He gestured to the shrub behind me.

I mishandled in the greenery for a stone and heaved it at him.

He intentionally let go of the rope and I went one more foot up. Just my shoulder bones on the ground when he got it once more. "Presently does that truly appear to be savvy?"

I frowned at him. "What are you doing, Jaecar!"

He whirled his wrist in the rope and slid close enough to turn me and squat by my face, bringing down my feet and lifting the log behind him. "I let you know I doing. Did you truly figure you could run? From me?"

"I truly think none about this can be occurring. It's wrong! You can't have me! You don't need me!" I struggled.

His forehead sewed as he gradually turned until his head was so topsy turvy as mine to give me a curious look. "Could it be said that you are distraught or blind?"

"This is rubbish!" I threw my arms.

"What, persay, is rubbish?"

"All of this!" I rolled sideways to grab the blade from his hip. Cutting the rope on my lower leg in a solitary movement and arriving on my feet. The meat actually held in my other hand.

He serenely stood and gave me an alerted look.

"I've cautioned you once. You'll not get one more from me." He intentionally shook his head.

Chapter 7
EveryWhere I'd Hide

I put his sharp edge in the abdomen of my dress and escaped back toward the town.

"Truly, Sam?" He shouted toward me.

Truly, Jaecar. You charlatan.

You're very much like them afterall!

He hadn't moved to seek after me and I considered returning to the cottage. Realizing now he'd disposed of it from his rundown of spots to search for me. However, I realized he wouldn't be a long ways behind.

I'll never make it that far.

What's more who's to say who else I may run into? Evening was coming fast.

The sun was high. Into the evening as of now. I could feel a trickle of hot perspiration sliding into my cleavage. I hustled through the trees.

Soothed at seeing my cottonwood. I did a handstand against it, actually gripping the meat in my shut clench hand, as I hurled my weight with brutal strength. Collapsing my feet into the convict and dropping them over the edge. Letting the heaviness of my legs drag me into this greater empty.

Tragically, this one was chest level with Jaecar and far more extensive. However, when I stow away in these trees I was undetectable. Nobody can track down me

I bowed my knees however much the tree would permit and shifted to the side of the opening, realizing my face wouldn't be apparent in obscurity internal parts of the tree.

I'd scarcely eaten down the pieces of meat when dim male hands came to inside the storage compartment and caught me by my armpit and hair to crease my head out of the opening and afterward my shoulders to yank me out.

He casually dropped me to the soil and leaves. Fierceness composed over his face. He got my arms and whirled me on the leaves. Mounting my hips in a jump and dropping intensely on me.

No moving away this time.

Chapter 8

Ravenous Males

He stuck one of my lower arms under every one of his knees. His weight making his bone press into the delicate tissues of my arm.

Oof!

"The Hell I'm not." He mumbled. Adjusting as he rode my midriff. Untwisting the rope and pulled his knife from the bind at my midriff to cut it into four pieces which he spread out close to us. Before intentionally pushing it back in his hip sheath.

"Jaecar!" I argued. "This is me we're discussing. You and I have been companions for eternity!"

Have you flown off the handle?

"Indeed. Furthermore currently we will be more. Substantially more." He declared.

"You would rather not mate with me!" I cried. "This is craziness."

He stopped with cutting the last piece of rope to gaze at me with wide eyes. "Will you truly be that unaware?"

"What?"

"One of the most impressive wolves in this pack has been sitting and perusing with you, going over your portrayals, discussing your speculations and taking strolls with you virtually consistently for quite a long time and you've not gotten on?"

"What are you saying?" I looked at him suspiciously.

"For what reason would I sit around doing that with a female I would have rather not breed?"

"What!" I gazed at him. Evidently my injuring was noticeable all over.

"No, it's not by any means the only explanation I become a close acquaintence with you. Stop it! There is nothing off about a physically fit male wanting his female of decision."

Then, at that point, he wavered aside to free one arm. Then, at that point, the alternate way for the other. Getting them individually and sticking them over my head to tie them in master hitches.

Being a Border Guard, he'd taken detainees previously.

Furthermore he knows how to get one.

He's getting me like one. I watched what he was doing to me in dismay.

He integrated my elbows across my stomach to restrict my battling.

My legs were straightaway. At my lower legs and simply over my knees.

Then, at that point, he lifted me and took me to the emptied out tree and slid me down into it.

It should've occurred to me he'd think that I'm in that tree. I used to stow away from him in it when we played.

I should've known better.

It was limited sufficient I slipped inside and arrived on my bound feet. I was battling and elbowing the two sides of the tree however could scarcely move.

He lifted a piece of wood which impeccably paired the tree. Eyeholes cut from knotholes that were unequivocally level with my eyes so I could look out, later he set it in the opening.

Be that as it may, Jaecar didn't be anything if not famously exact.

Viably impeding me from view and hooking it set up with something outwardly.

My stomach sank as I understood the total utter haziness. Furthermore how this affected me. I'd not be in the security of my hovel as the moon rose this evening. I'll be defenseless and uncovered.

Each component, the breeze and downpour would convey my female fragrance to the greedy guys.

Chapter 9
Wait Quietly

Jaecar's light green eyes showed up in my line of vision. "Sit tight for me." He said. "Discreetly."

My lips jerked in hatred as I scowled at him.

"Keep in mind, assuming you shout, on the off chance that you battle, the pack will hear you."

Also they'll all need to mate. I knew it without him saying it.

I saw my plain dress was torn close to my knees and smirched across the chest.

I'm foul. I thought bluntly.

Agonizing over inconsequential things appeared to make the truth of my treachery disappear.

I realized sunset was coming since I could hear the howls and wails of the more youthful guys that had surrendered to the change immediately.

Will they aroma me. I speculated Jaecar had done his exploration and realized that encased in the tree they'd be unable to follow my aroma. Regardless of whether they get it, it's far-fetched they'll track down me

Yet, I'd been off-base previously.

I could hear the first wheezing as the sun was setting. A wolf had followed me over here and was heaving close to the tree.

"Move away!" I heard Jaecar's voice. Snarling in hazardous notice. Then, at that point, I heard a crash and the sound of bones crunching.

A howl showing the wolf was harmed.

Jaecar ventured into view and conveyed one more savage kick to the wolves ribs. "Leave!" He ground out. "My region!"

The wolf gave a piercing cry and walked from my view.

Jaecar's eyes were level with the peepholes again yet I could see now they were slitted.

He's wild at this point. I could tell just from taking a gander at him. I'd never seen him like this.

Consistently before I'd secured myself in the hovel and he'd assisted me with invigorating it and put on the additional locks so no measure of charging or delving would get the wolves into my area.

Consistently I was protected. As a result of him.

Presently I would be...Because of him? It had some issues. It seemed like the most unimaginable selling out.

He thumped aside the piece of wood obstructing the opening and his arms ventured into overlap me back through the opening and haul me out.

"Jaecar!" I was practically glad to be liberated from the tree. Figuring I could convince him to release me. I threw my red-light hair as he set me on the ground. Stooping so he could change his stance and lift me into his arms.

He strolled a brief distance and I heard the wolves crying somewhere out there.

They can smell me now. I looked around his arm yet couldn't see any yet.

We arrived at a swinging wood and rope scaffold and I was terrified.

In any case, as he did all things, Jaecar crossed it expertly. Surefooted and impeccably adjusted.

Which is the way he wins each competition.

He wasn't enormous like a portion of the others however he was tall, wide carried, flexible and staggeringly spry.

All of which bode sick for me now.

Chapter 10

A StrongHold

Jaecar strolled into a bungalow inside the trees. An invigorated development I hadn't known was here. He kicked the entryway shut. Turning, he tipped me up to lift his arm sufficiently high he could hold and turn the locks.

"What is this spot?"

"My home." He set me on the mat while he hunched to get a fire rolling. "You cold?"

I was. Yet, I wasn't going to concede shortcoming to him. Not this evening. It'd just make his hunter sense more fierce. I knew enough with regards to wolves to realize that.

"Fine." He shrugged when I didn't reply.

He got the fire rolling and attempted to loosen my lower legs. Holding them together as he sat on them to fix the limiting at my knees and climbed to ride my abdomen. "Sam, I really want you to coordinate."

"I won't, Jaecar. I didn't consent to this."

"No you didn't. I gave you time. Furthermore openings. Yet, I'm apprehensive in a couple of hours you will not have a decision. I will take you."

A shudder moved down my spine. "You wouldn't."

"I will. I'm going to." He said solidly. Lips fixing. "I've didn't consider anything else. Also I'm reluctant to stand by any more drawn out. I've guarded you." He gestured back toward where my cottage, my safe-haven was. "From them. From me. However, it's time that you let it go. That you comprehend you will be my mate."

"I won't." I shook my head resolutely.

"I was apprehensive you'd say that." He murmured. As he loosened up the limiting at my elbows and got my wrists. Lifting them over my head to drop over a snare in the floor which confronted away from me. Then, at that point, he slid down and got my lower legs to pull me down level on the floor covering. Yanking the rope restricting my wrists tight and immediately causing me to feel helpless.

Frantic.

"Jaecar. Jaecar, please!"

Try not!

"Quit saying my name." he snarled. Hanging over me. "It's making me harder."

I consented. Eyes wide. As my look meandered his attractive face. I couldn't resist the urge to attempt once again. "Try not to do this..."

He was so wonderful. Penetrating green eyes. Sparkling dark hair which cleared back from his face and along his head to clear his collar. A straight, haughty, nose and enticing lips.

How is it that he could be so pitiless?

He snorted and abruptly hung over me to crush his hips into my midsection. Growling in a wolf's voice.

Disquiet was settling through me. The Mating Moon is rising.

I need to move away!

Jaecar drew my underpants down, stopping to finger the subsequent belt.

Realizing I generally wear two to forestall this. How frequently had I trusted that to him?

He viewed at me as his unpleasant knuckles brushed along my exposed thighs. He threw my clothing into the fire.

A work to conceal my fragrance.

Different wolves would follow my smell to this cabin.

Furthermore they'll attempt to get in. Get to me...

He snarled eagerly prior to requesting. "Keep still."

He loosened his calfskin pants and liberated what I dreaded the most.

Chapter 11

In His Domain

Panic was setting in and I lurched up to escape him.

Twisting my thighs to get away.

His hands landed on them. Fingers biting to keep them in place.

TO KEEP ME IN PLACE.

"Sam!" He commanded. "This is happening. I can be gentle if you don't resist."

He pushed my thighs apart and landed over me in a pushup. Making it impossible to close my legs since he already lay between them.

"You're not doing this to me!" I jerked against the ropes. They bit into my skin but wouldn't relent.

"Don't make me tie down your legs." He warned.

I paused. Considering if he'd really do it. But there was a hard glint in his eyes I'd never seen before. *He absolutely will.*

He slowly lifted my skirt. Looking almost apologetically into my eyes as he straightened the hem across his chest. Fisting two edges before jerking violently and tearing it up the front. It caught at my waist.

I shrieked at the sudden brutality.

"Ssh." He whispered. Sliding until his groin pressed mine while he caught the shoulders of my plain, white gown. Shredding it down to my waist, exposed my breasts to the cool night air.

I was impossibly vulnerable. *Free for the taking without my clothes.*

"Jaecar!" I cried.

He grabbed the thick ribbon cinching my waist and broke it off me. Peeling my dress apart to expose my body.

Groaning in arousal. "I'm going to enter you now, Sam."

He reached down between us and his fingers stroked my lower lips. Then a finger crept into me and I felt myself stretching to accommodate the intrusion.

When I objected again, he balled the bit of ribbon in his free hand and reached up to push it into my mouth. "Now be quiet lest you summon the pack before I can seed you."

I FEARED I KNEW WHAT HE MEANT.

I tried to make sounds around the ribbon but it'd soaked all moisture from my mouth and kept my teeth pried open and my tongue locked to the bottom of my mouth.

When he knew I was wet, Jaecar removed his finger and caught himself in his hands. Brushing along my entrance.

He felt hard as a rod and far too big to fit in me.

I was arching up. My heels skidding along the rug as I tried to writhe away.

He entered me and the sensation was so sudden that I stilled. Afraid I'd be hurt if I kept struggling. Inch by inch, he was inside me. Moaning as he struggled to control the animal inside him.

"The moon is almost up, Sam. I won't have control then. My body will take yours. I'm trying to heat you first."

WHAT DID THAT MEAN?

Once all the way inside me, my body reacted by biting down on him.

He shouted in pleasure and pushed hard. Feeling the entrance of my cervix deep in me.

I lurched up to ease the pressure but his hands snatched my hips and thudded them roughly back to the floor. With an animalistic snarl, he drove in viciously. Pumping into me once, twice, three times. Moaning in pleasure as he moved within me.

My efforts to wiggle away seemed to stimulate him. Growling low in his throat he grew more violent.

One hand held my hip against him. The other scooped a small pert breast. Fingers smashing into the firmness. Massaging it as roughly as he massaged my inner walls.

"Sam!"

Chapter 12
Skin on Skin

His muscled buttocks flexed as he probed deep beneath my stomach. Making me shout around the ribbon in my mouth.

There was hot moistness deep in me and I suddenly knew this was what he meant by 'seeding.'

He'd filled my body with his pleasure.

Grunting he collapsed over me. His knees drawing up on each side of my hips. Making my legs drape his sinewed thighs. He summoned enough strength to pull his tunic over his head. Yanking his pants further down his thighs. He lay atop me.

His length still firmly inside me as he fell momentarily asleep.

Our skin meshed, along the length of my body. Both inside and outside of me. *Utterly possessing my flesh. Invading me in every way he could.*

I managed to spit out the ribbon. Feeling the ache inside me. The stretching where he was fitted into me. I tried to move to ease the tenseness of my muscles. *Trying to push him out.*

But his reaction was volatile. He snapped to full wakefulness.

And hardness.

Jamming violently into me until his hips burrowed into my thighs.

I shouted and tried to twist sideways and get my legs around him. Trying to kick him back.

But he growled low in his throat. His chest shining with the sweat generated by his rising heat. His abdomen clenching as he felt my inner muscles sucking on him.

He jerked my shoulder back and shoved my back flat on the floor. Leaning forward to straighten his legs between mine.

I was shocked at how deep he was suddenly in me. Touching low behind my belly. The weight of his body pushing on the surface of my pelvis to compress him inside me. Adding pressure to the movement of the mushroom shape topping his staff.

He was so deep.

"I can't take anymore of it." I objected. Starting to sweat at the hint of pain as he thrust in and out. And in again. Harder each time, so my body jerked. Sliding on the rug with the impact.

"You can." He croaked in a dry voice. "And you will. Again and again."

He sounds like he means it.

"Your body..." He said in pleasure. Stroking in and out. "It loves the way I feel. Your so wet. The inside of you is sucking on my cock. Pulling me deeper."

"I can't take you any deeper!"

His weight was pinning me to the floor. His hands cupped my breasts between us. And his mouth found mine. His tongue intruding in my mouth and matching the violent pace of his stem stabbing inside me.

"You bastard!" I twisted my face away.

"I'm rising again." He slammed hard into me and held it a moment then slipped it out and back in with two more hard thrusts. Emptying his seed deep in my womb.

"Your body is mine now." He panted as he laid back on me. His forehead resting on the wood next to my head.

"Please stop!"

"No." He shook his head. "You're mine tonight. I'll take my pleasure from you and give you yours, and in the morning I'll mark you as mine. No other man will touch you after that. Only I will ever feel you."

I shook my head. "Not after this. Now I'll find another man. I'll never be your mate. I may give to the pack what you had to steal, just to wash away what you've done!"

Chapter 13

Paying for My Insult

He reared back as though I'd hit him. "The Hell if you think so!" His feral eyes narrowed on me. "I was being kind, but you'll pay for saying that. You'll ache tomorrow. I'm going to fuck you until all you feel is me in your body with every step you take. To remind you who you belong to!"

"No!"

"Yes." He withdrew to slam back into me. Intent on showing me my place.

I yelped against the stretching and the ache in me.

He sat back on his haunches and tossed one of my legs over his head. Rolling me onto my stomach made the rope on my wrists tighten.

I felt cold wood under my breasts and against my flat belly. *What's he going to do to me now?*

I knew a moment of deep fear as I felt the weight of his rod sliding along my crack. I feared for one horrible moment, he'd hurt me in truth.

Instead he adjusted me and entered me again. It was so abrupt that I launched forward to get away from him.

"On your knees." He shouted. Hauling me back by my hips to sit on my heels and his lap.

In an effort to assuage the pressure at my core I quickly obeyed, hoping to get get off him some.

But he followed me up. Rising to his knees. He pushed a palm between my shoulders so my breasts and chin were back on the floor. My ass high up for the taking. He was already planted in me and moaning in pleasure but at this angle he could lean over my back and put his hands parallel to my shoulder. Thrusting hard into me.

"Jaecar please!" I begged. "You're hurting me!"

"Maybe you'll learn then what you don't say to your mate." He pumped harder. Grunting with each thrust. Pleasure surging through him and super heating his body.

I realized that in this position, he was taking me like a wolf. *Mounting me.*

And from the sounds he made it appeared he enjoyed it. "You love this, don't you!" I accused.

"You bound and submitting?" He laughed. "Yes I do." One hand lifted to leverage my hip in place. His weight increasing to keep me from moving as he pulsed into me. "Spilling into you again and again. Yes I do." He groaned. "Utterly possessing you? Yes!"

"You're the devil!" I wailed.

"And you'll learn to take it. And to enjoy it. You're my mate, Sam."

Chapter 14

Open For Him

BETRAYAL. That was all I could think.

He'd betrayed me. I barely woke from subsiding into an exhausted collapse. Avoiding the new pain. When I did, I found I was tied face down over the back of a wooden chair. I tried to move and figured out my ankles were each bound to a chair leg. I was tipped over the back of the chair, so it dug into my stomach. Each of my wrists tied to a front leg of the chair.

I tried to move but every pull tugged at something else. Yanking my arms strained my ankles and vice versa. The ropes were so tight they bit into my skin.

"You're awake." I heard Jaecar's voice from behind me and had to lean to look around my own leg to see him sitting there against the wall. Boots crossed at his ankle. Wearing only them and his leather pants. Tossing chunks of meat from a platter into his mouth as he leisurely took in the sight of me so vulnerable.

"Please let me go." I gave him a desperate look.

"Why would I do that?" He threw another bite of meat in his mouth. Gesturing. "I like you like this."

BENT OVER A CHAIR. READY TO BE HIS UNWILLING PLAYTHING.

"Besides," He stood up and dusted off his hands, heading for me. "I'm not nearly done with you."

He looked so calm. His shirt gone and the front of his black leather pants unlaced and hanging open. Revealing his upper pelvis and pubic line. The deep 'v' of muscle cutting down from his hips to where I knew his cock was nestled. He strolled up behind me and I fought against the chair. My breasts bobbing as I jerked left and right up and down.

He chuckled from behind me. Slapping my ass and watching hungrily as it bounced slightly. Then he pushed his crotch against me. I felt the lacings of his breeches against my opening. He cupped the bottom of each of my buttocks,

clawing them slightly as his grip slid up. He growled
lasciviously.

He's going to take me again.

Chapter 15

His Vengeance

I heard him tugging at the laces to loosen his pants and slide
them down.

There was a long moment where I felt nothing. Twisting to
see, I could catch just enough movement to know he was
stroking himself.

"You look amazing this way. I'm going to be hard pressed to
ever untie you." He purred.

He entered me.

Making me give a broken scream at the sudden pain. The unexpected stretching as my body accommodated his length. I instantly knew this discomfort would make everything more intense. The chair back pinching into my abdomen compressed my entryway making stretching around him even tighter.

He groaned and pushed past the compression. Shaking as he drug it back. Feeling my body biting down on him in surprise, had him moaning in pleasure as he stroked my back. Moving methodically into me.

"I don't want this, Jaecar."

"I didn't ask what you wanted."

"You don't want to do this to me." I tried a different tactic. Trying to reach the man I'd known the last few years.

If he's even still in there.

If he was ever real...

"Oh, I very much do. Every day. For the rest of my life. Harder." He slammed in. "And harder." He pushed deep. Growling in passion. "And harder." He was pumping into me. Surging like a rutting animal. Gripping the chair back

for leverage, he curled his abdomen to get more of an
upward angle. Scraping against the surfaces in me before
bending to penetrate me bent over as I was.

He slapped my buttocks again.

Startled I clenched around him.

He moaned. "Oh, yeah...that feels good."

He slapped me again and again I tightened. His excitement
made him drive into me wildly. His sack slapping against my
upper lips as he thrust. "You feel so good. This, warm place
is mine. All mine."

Chapter 16

Dominating Me for His Pleasure

"No!" I shouted in sudden indignation. Infuriated that he cared so little what I wanted.

He paused to tilt sideways and challenge me. "Say 'no' to me again."

He was still planted in me and his threat was clear but my pride drove me. "You can go to hell! I'm not yours. I'm going to fuck all of them."

"Then why shouldn't I open the door and let them line up to have you now. You're open and ready and they'd all love a go at you. Taking you like animals. Spilling seed into you until you were heavy with a pack pup." His shoulders heaved with rage.

"One after another they'd have a go at you. Perhaps it's what you deserve!" He slid out of me and walked to the door. Flipping the locks and putting his palm on the handle.

Closing my eyes, I surrendered. "No. Fine, Jaecar."

"Fine what?" His eyes were zeroed in on me. Lip curled in disdain.

"My body is yours. Tonight."

"I'll take that." He flipped all the locks back into place. "For now."

Returning, he grabbed the chair back and his thighs hit the back of me as he slammed into me.

I yelped.

"Don't ever again tell me you'll fuck another male."

"Okay…" I sobbed. Wanting to hide my face.

He pounded into me relentlessly. Ruthlessly owning my body. My breasts bounced at the force of every thrust. "Yes. Oh, you feel fantastic. Take it. Take my cock. Take it deep."

WHAT CHOICE DID I HAVE?

"Tell me you love it." He suddenly commanded.

"I don't."

He tipped the chair back toward him and brought my ass slamming back against him and the upward angle of my weight pressing me firmly onto his rock solid cock. Making me plead his name again. Desperately clawing the chair to try and evade how deeply he was settled in.

He wasn't moving, just enjoying the press of his cock burrowing into the entrance of my womb while I writhed to get away.

"I love it." I surrendered.

He slammed the chair back to all four legs and commenced bouncing into me forcefully. His gleeful moans rising in crescendo until I felt him swelling even more within my walls then the hot spill of his liquids into me.

He shouted in pleasure. "The bed next!" He commanded. "I'm going to fuck you over the edge of the bed until you can't walk!"

Chapter 17

Avoiding a Worse Brutality

Despite what he'd said, he stood there panting. Catching his breath. And he slumped over me. His chest resting along my spine and him still implanted in me. His sweating arms framing mine and he rubbed his roughened palms up and down my arms.

"Sam..."

"Don't say my name." I shook my head angrily.

"Don't talk to me like that." He said softly. Commanding voice gone.

"Like what now, Jaecar?"

"Like you hate me."

"I do."

"You don't hate me." He said sadly. Straightening and stroking a palm down my spine. "You're angry and wounded by what I'm doing to you."

"I'm all of those things." I tugged at the bindings on my wrist. Jerking forcefully. I realized my mistake when I felt him swelling within my swore walls again. Stretching me.

"Not again..." I pleaded. "A break."

"I can't." His face crunched with his effort to stay himself. He gave a roar that was the cry of his beast. Thrusting wildly into me again. Delving in madly. Tipping the chair back against the crook of him he spurred in, in short quick jerks.

I was uttering a low vibrating moan against the sensation. A strange friction building with the ache. And the stabbing pains. He let go of the chair to hold me by my hips. Keeping them planted against him. While he did short up thrusts. Moaning and sweating as he writhed into me. Angling me to accept his length. Feeling his muscular thighs pumping as he buried himself in the cushion of my body.

"Jaecar..." I wailed.

"Soon." He grunted. Slamming the chair down and leaning to wind his arm in my long red-blonde hair. Using it for leverage to pound into me.

"Uh. Uh." He threw his head back. Shouting my name as he came. Burrowed in my heat.

Grunting in frustration at himself. He stretched over me and quickly unlaced the ropes binding my wrists to the chair. Lacing them together.

He withdrew from me with a pleasured gasp. Crouching weakly to untie my ankles.

Standing, he let me catch my breath, slumped over the chair but without being stretched open.

He shucked his pants and kicked them aside. Walking round the chair and catching the rope binding my wrists to lead me to the bed.

"I can't." I whined. "I'm so tired."

"Do you ache?" He asked.

"Yes."

"Does it feel like I'm still planted in you?"

I nodded. Thinking I might get a hint of sympathy.

"Good. I want it to hurt to walk tomorrow. I want everything to hurt. So you can't pretend like it never happened."

I should've known better then to hope for some compassion.

"What's wrong with you?" I asked his back. "Why have you turned on me?"

He stopped and went rigid. Without turning he said, "Do you know that Draven is seeking a mate tonight?"

My eyes widened. *He's a known brute. Nearly feral.*

"What if he'd chosen you, Sam? What then?"

"Would he have done to me what you have?" I demanded. Mouth white.

"Worse. He's relentless. And his stamina and imagination far surpass mine. You'd likely not have survived him."

As much as I hated what he was saying, I suspected he was right. *Damn him!*

Chapter 18

What Do You Want

Jaecar pushed me down to kneel next to the bed. Tying my wrists to the headboard.

I whimpered. Exhausted and so sore I just wanted to squeeze my thighs together and cradle myself. I couldn't take much more.

"I'm not your plaything." I moaned into the blankets.

"I know." He said, surprisingly. Leaning over my back and sweeping my hair over one shoulder to kiss the side of my neck and shoulder. Reaching around to cup the weight of my breasts.

I shuddered because I feared it would arouse him again and start the whole brutal process once more.

But he tenderly molded the soft tissue. Framing them with his large palms. Learning the feel and texture. He kissed down my back. Gripping my waist. I could feel his need already raging through him.

It's nearly midnight. The Mating Moon was in full power.

It was shocking he'd not already changed to mount me as an animal. Forcing me to change by the sheer hormones he'd generate as the beast.

He's trying to control it.

"Why aren't you changing?" I asked, my voice muffled in the bed.

"I'm trying not to hurt you anymore than necessary."

"Why? You don't seem to even care."

He scooped my shins and tossed me on the bed in a ball. Turning me onto my back and unfolding me. Straddling my legs and laying atop me. Continuing his soft ministrations to my chest as he scented my neck. Whispering. "You're wrong."

"What do you want from me?"

"You know." He groaned helplessly. Lifting one hand to twine in my hair. "I'd never have wished to hurt you. I didn't want you to see this side of what we are."

"That's why you fortified my hut?"

He swallowed hard. His jaw ticking next to my cheek. "I wanted inside it. In you. Every Mating Moon. Enough I'd have been the first one to tear your hut apart if I hadn't...and violently mount you."

"So, why now?" I looked sadly at his face. The face of the one I'd trusted most. The man who'd spent all of this day tormenting me.

"Because I've the most control, I'll ever have on my beast. And Draven spoke of taking a mate tonight. And because the pack had set me the ultimatum of breeding you or luring you out for them to have you."

"That would've been horrible." I admitted. Staring at the ceiling as I fought tears.

"More horrible than this?" He caressed one of my cheeks with his thumb. Giving me a wounded look.

And I realized his deep conflict. Knowing that with the scent I was generating tonight there's no way he could've resisted me.

If he'd have chained himself to a wall, he'd have snapped them to enter me. But knowing it didn't make it any less painful mentally or physically.

"I know you don't understand." He read my face. Burying his mouth in my shoulder. Moaning as he writhed against my belly. Stroking himself against my bare abdomen and shaking from the pressure of it. "I can't control it much longer..."

"Please don't hurt me anymore." I whispered.

He lifted his head at my barely whispered words.

I gave him a desperate look.

"Then you mount me."

Chapter 19

Making Me Ride Him

"I-I don't know how..." I confided.

"I know."

I somehow knew it was still going to hurt. *No matter what it was going to. I was raw and exhausted.*

"I'll teach you but we have to be quick."

"Will you let me go?"

"Not a chance." His eyes narrowed on me.

"Afraid of me getting away?"

"More afraid of you running out naked in the night and being pounced on by the pack."

That thought was unbearable. I winced at the imagery.

"I won't."

"Sure, you won't." Disbelief was written over his face. "I know you well, Sam. You'd do anything to get away from me now."

He wasn't wrong.

But better the devil I now knew then the multiple ones I did not.

He climbed over me, to shift a lever on the wall.

Chains lowered from a pulley above. Dropping several feet over our heads.

"Chains?" I yelped.

Iron shackles swayed on the end of them.

"Over your bed? Why?"

He winced. Jaw tightening. "For you. I knew you'd fight."

I stared at them in horror.

"Thought the ropes might be a bit easier to take."

"Neither is easy to take. None of this is."

"I understand." He gingerly guided me up onto my heels.
Clicking the shackle over the rope between my wrists and
taking the key to set on the chair.

Out of my reach.

I swallowed. Scared of what he'd tell me to do. Afraid of how
much it would hurt. And petrified of how vulnerable it'd
make me.

With every step he grunted and thrusted against air.
Fighting his beast. Sniffing the air, he'd groan in
pain. *Catching my scent.*

He pushed me aside so he could lay on his back on the bed.
Staring up at me. He grabbed one of my thighs in a shaking
hand. "I'm trying, Sam. But I'm losing it. You're going to
have to take it."

Take over the joining?

He guided my thigh over him so I hovered above his
straining length. The swollen part of him begging for relief.
"God..." He groaned. "I can feel the heat your emitting and
your smell..." He gave a pained moan.

His hips started to lift and he forced them back into the bed. Away from me.

His control is waning. He wanted to lurch up into me.

"Lower yourself, Samantha."

I gave him a puzzled look.

He pointed at the inch apart we were from him entering me.

Chewing my cheek, I slid my knees apart. Hissing in pain at the sting of moving to open myself. The motion lowered me over him. I paused when the tip of him began opening the bruised lips of my opening. Parting them as they licked at his length.

He arched up. Throwing his head back. But when he'd have driven deep in me, I leapt up and out of his reach.

"Samantha!" He snarled. His hands gripping my thighs in a biting grip. Knowing if he shoved them down it would plant me on his root.

Chapter 20

What He's Done To Me All Night

His thumbs flexed along my skin and I could see the anguish written over his face. His sex pulsed against me and his body flushed. Veins in his neck rising as he strained against the brutal beast wanting to be unleashed.

"Sam!"

I took sympathy on him and slid back down. Inching over him.

He fisted the bedding. Grunting ferociously and writhing to keep from violently pumping into me. Once I felt him completely sheltered in my body, I tested the feel of him by lightly flexing the places where I was so sore.

My walls grabbed him like a fist and the reaction was volatile. His knees drew up against my back. His abdomen tightened in rippling muscles. Long sinews crossed his chest and his arms flexed. He roared through his teeth. Hovering his hands outside my hips.

In agony.

I slid my knees in toward his ribs. Framing his sides with my calves.

He reached to the outside of them and pulled them tight against him. Giving me a wide-eyed look as he panted.

I slid upward and he clenched. His head rolling back and throat bowing up as he flexed. Wanting to follow me to sink deep again.

I slowly lowered back down feeling a delicious flexing. Even in my sore places. Everything stretched around him more easily and I began to slide up and down more quickly. Keeping from bouncing against him because my entrance was swollen and tender.

He was grunting. Moaning everytime I sucked him in again. I began pushing forward with my hips as I lowered to see what it did and he sat up to cup my breasts.

It changed the angle immediately. Pushing more toward the back.

And he was suddenly inches from my face. He brushed his lips over mine as I moved atop him.

My body covered in goosebumps. He cupped my breasts and caressed them. Thumbing my nipples made me rear forward on him and he hissed through his teeth and flexed into me. Unable to resist grabbing my hips and forcing me down hard on him as he strained to burrow into me. I felt his thighs and hips shivering. He shouted almost as if in pain. Then his head fell back and he shouted again through gritted teeth and I felt the hot surge of warmth seeping into me and rolling back down to heat his length.

I relaxed and slumped down on him.

With him still planted in me. He tossed his head. Trying to resist forcing another climax instantly.

Suddenly my body had a violent reaction. My spine jerked taut and I thrust up my breasts. My belly tightening in a white hot explosion where I grabbed him inside and held him. Grasping him in clenching pulses that had him whooshing quick breaths and his hands hovering as he floundered. His face crumpled as he fought for control.

I howled in pleasure. Feeling my body spasming and a sudden chill freezing my skin. I looked at him in wonder. "What was that?"

He threw his forearm over his eyes as he struggled to hold still. "It's what I've been doing all night."

Chapter 21

Primal Reaction

"That is the thing that it seems like." He clarified. "No. It's likely more extreme for me since it is a help to the frenzied need."

"For what reason aren't you checking out me?" I was a little injured that he didn't wish to see what I'd encountered.

"Since seeing you pleasuring yourself by utilizing my body is damn close to making me insane. My wolf is prepared to detonate."

"Then, at that point, do it." I murmured. Needing to return that upbeat happiness he'd recently offered me.

His arm fell away and he lifted his head to give me a bewildered look. "What?"

"Release him. I need to meet him."

"For what reason would you need that?"

"Since it is the thing that we are and mine needs a greater amount of what she recently had."

He gazed at me mouth agape. "Indeed ma'am."

He slid sideways off the bed. Unfastening my wrists and freely restricting the rope around his abdomen and mine. Binding us together at the abdomens.

I gave him a scrutinizing investigate my shoulder.

"I can't chance you surging out there." He motioned to the entryway.

Be that as it may, it would mean he could remain mounted in me throughout the evening. I gave him a since a long time ago stressed look.

As usual, he read my face. "I may. I can't handle how my wolf will deal with yours under a Mating Moon. You sure this is what you need?"

"Do I have a decision?"

"I'm attempting to give you one."

"Be that as it may, you will transform into a wolf?"

"Indeed." He conceded. Moaning. "Furthermore I will check you, Sam. You're mine. I'll never impart you to another. I need to be the main one to offer you this. Yet, I would like to show you it doesn't need to be enduring and torment. I'll allow you to have your direction with my body, hurt me, until you can trust me once more."

"Yet, I detected there was a trick.

"Yet, every Mating Moon...I will claim you. Completely have your body. Associating on our most base level."

Chapter 22

Marking Me

I cycle my lip.

"In any case, the aggravation will reduce, I promise it." He attempted to console. Articulation thoughtful.

He's stressed I'll battle him.

Yet, as insufferable as this night had been. I realized it could've been more terrible because of another man. I knew another would've broken my body. Left my soul destroyed. And all with as little inclination as having spit on me.

Dreadful as he was, Jaecar needed to be my mate. He had shielded me from this dim piece of being a wolf for quite a long time.

I loathed him. In any case, I really focused on him.

At the point when he directed me to sit straight where we bowed together, and put a hand to my jaw to turn my face, he kissed me all the more delicately then I'd at any point have speculated anybody could.

I could feel my posterior pushing on his masculinity. Where he was at that point hard once more. Needing inside me.

He was growling. A low thunder of expectation arising out of his chest.

Eager to fill me once more.

I inclined forward and arranged my opening on him and I brought down leisurely back on him. Offering my irritated body a chance to extend around him. Changing in accordance with fit him perfectly.

He had a white knuckled grasp on the edge of the bed.

"What are you doing?" I sat mounted on him and didn't move. Profoundly satisfied, in a way I'd never concede, that I realized I was breaking his iron-clad control.

"Attempting " Grunt. "to keep from-" Grunt. "beating you until you breakdown."

I focused on my internal dividers and violently flexed them.

Breaking his control and unchaining his monster.

He utilized up into me and squeezed my hips into the edge of
the bed. Siphoning into me in short quick strokes. Squeezing
a bosom and partaking in the manner it ricocheted into his
palm. His other one wrapped my throat and pulled me
against his chest. Curving my back as he push into me.

Snorting viciously as he had his direction with my body.

He squeezed a fast kiss to my lips. Hide was following over
both our arms and I felt it isolating my pores to trail my
spine. I felt the sinking of his teeth on the rear of my
shoulder. Profoundly inserting and holding tight as he
worked into me. Tunneling further with each amazing
stroke. Accomplishing more uplifted delight.

I groaned as that white-hot blast blew behind my eyes.
Sending my body in wild spasms.

His as well. The two of us had become wolves. Taking joy from every others tissue.

Furthermore that was the manner by which my companion had turned into my awful, unpredictable mate.

I hope you like my this book.

So please review and comment this book...

THANK YOU //